RATATATTATATATTATATAT!

I never dreamed feet could make so much noise!

"Those tap shoes are the best," I whispered to Emma. "If I had those, I would tap twenty-four hours a day!"

"You should take tap dance with me," Emma whispered back. "We'd have so much fun together!"

My very own noisy shoes?

"Emma," I said, "you are a genius."

ROSCOE RILEY

Rules

#5

Don't Tap-Dance on Your Teacher

Katherine Applegate
illustrated by Brian Biggs

HarperTrophy®
An Imprint of HarperCollinsPublishers

For the Dusek clan

Harper Trophy® is a registered trademark of
HarperCollins Publishers.
Roscoe Riley Rules #5: Don't Tap-Dance
on Your Teacher
Text copyright © 2009 by Katherine Applegate
Illustrations copyright © 2009 by Brian Biggs
For information address HarperCollins
Children's Books, a division of HarperCollins
Publishers, 10 East 53rd Street, New York,
NY 10022.
www.harpercollinschildrens.com

Library of Congress Cataloging-in-Publication Data
Applegate, Katherine.
Don't tap-dance on your teacher / by Katherine
Applegate. — 1st ed.
    p. cm. — (Roscoe Riley rules ; #5)
    Summary: Roscoe cannot wait to tap dance in the
school talent show until some older boys make fun
of him and say that tap dancing is just for girls.
    ISBN 978-0-06-114889-7 (pbk. bdg.)
    ISBN 978-0-06-114890-3 (trade bdg.)
    [1. Tap dancing—Fiction. 2. Talent shows—Fiction.
3. Self-confidence—Fiction. 4. Schools—Fiction.
5. Humorous stories.] I. Title. II. Title: Do not tap-
dance on your teacher.
PZ7.A6483Dot 2009   2008022378
[Fic]—dc22   CIP
                                                   AC

            09 10 11 12 13 LP/CW 10 9 8 7 6 5 4 3 2
                                ❖
                          First Edition

572 4975

Contents

#5

Don't Tap-Dance
on Your Teacher

1
Welcome to Time-Out

I can guess what you're thinking.

Time-out AGAIN? What rule did you break this time, Roscoe?

Well, since you asked, it was Rule Number 542: DO NOT PRETEND TO NEED CRUTCHES WHEN YOU REALLY DO NOT NEED THEM JUST TO GET OUT OF AN EMBARRASSING SITUATION.

1

Personally, I don't think a guy should get punished for breaking a rule when he didn't even exactly know there *was* such a rule.

But my mom and dad see things a little differently.

Sometimes I wonder if they ever really were kids.

You'd think people who used to be kids would understand that sometimes a guy just really needs a good crutch. Or two.

You know what I'm talking about, right?

Well, maybe it is a *little* confusing.

I'll begin at the beginning of the beginning.

With my friend Emma's amazing, noisy shoes . . .

2

Something You Should Know
Before We Get Started

Mom says girls can do anything boys can do.

Dad says boys can do anything girls can do.

Probably they're right.

Parents usually are.

But somebody needs to make sure kids

3

hear this news.

Kids need to know there's no such thing as just-for-boys stuff and just-for-girls stuff.

Like for instance, dancing elephants can be boys or girls.

Dancing mice too.

3

Something Else
You Should Know
Before We Get Started

If you are pretending you smushed your leg, try to remember which leg is the limpy one and which one is not.

This advice may come in very handy someday.

4

Mr. Megaphone

The first time I heard Emma's tapping shoes was during show-and-tell.

Ms. Diz, my teacher, lets us bring all kinds of weird stuff to share with the class.

She is a brand-new teacher, so she likes to experiment on us.

Once Dewan brought a ferret. Which is

like a stretched-out guinea pig.

After that, Ms. Diz made up the No Show-and-Tells that Can Bite rule.

Maya brought her grandpa's artificial leg to another show-and-tell.

After that, Ms. Diz made up the No Show-and-Tells Without Permission of the Owner rule.

The same day Emma brought her new tap shoes to school, I brought something from my Noisy Stuff collection.

I always bring noisy stuff for show-and-tell.

I LOVE noise!

Weird noise.

Funny noise.

And of course, best of all, LOUD noise.

Here's what I've collected so far:

The newest addition to my Noisy Stuff collection is my Mr. Megaphone.

It looks like a giant ice-cream cone made of plastic.

When you talk into the mouth hole, it changes your voice so you sound like a megamonster.

A loud megamonster with a bad cold.

When it was my turn for show-and-tell, I yelled, "Take me to your leader, first grad-ers of the Earth!" into the megaphone.

Half the class covered their ears.

The other half went "WHOA!"

"Roscoe, that's a fine addition to your Noisy Stuff collection," Ms. Diz said. "Thank you for sharing it."

"I can pass it around," I offered.

"Please, NO!" Ms. Diz said. "I mean, we have other people who want to share this morning. Speaking of things that make noise, Emma, you have something special to show us today, don't you?"

Emma held up two black shoes with metal tappers on the bottom.

"These are my tap shoes," she said. "They make noise when you step."

Shoes with built-in noise? I thought. *What will they think of next?*

And that's how it all began.

5

The Amazing Coolness of Noisy Shoes

"I just had my first tap dance lesson yesterday," Emma said.

She put on the shoes. When she walked on the carpet, they just sounded like plain old everyday shoes.

But on the hard floor, an amazing thing happened!

Emma's feet went *click! click! click!*

Those tappers made some serious noise.

Emma tapped and twirled, and we all clapped for her.

"Amazing tapping, Earth girl," I said into my Mr. Megaphone.

"Very nice, Emma," said Ms. Diz. "And that's probably enough Mr. Megaphone for today, Roscoe. For the year, actually."

I put down the megaphone and raised my hand. "Can boys do tap dancing?" I asked.

Wyatt laughed. "Guys don't tap-dance," he said. "Guys do football and soccer."

"Girls can do soccer," Emma said.

Coco stood up. She put her hands on her hips. "Also, I would like to point out that girls rule and boys drool."

"Coco, please watch your words," Ms. Diz said.

Gus raised his hand. "Ms. Diz?" he said. "Dogs drool. Cats not so much."

"Thank you for that, Gus," said Ms. Diz. She took a deep breath.

She breathes a lot, actually.

14

"As it happens, Wyatt, there are many famous male tap dancers," said Ms. Diz. "And Emma is right. Some of the best soccer players in the world are girls."

She thought for a second. Then she snapped her fingers.

"There's something I want you all to see," Ms. Diz said. "I'll give Ms. Bunelli a quick call right now!"

Ms. Bunelli is the school media center specialist.

But she says just call her the Library Lady.

There are about a kazillion books and DVDs and cool things in the library. I do not know how she has time to keep track of them all.

I think maybe she never goes home.

A few minutes later, Ms. Bunelli came

to our class. She was rolling a tall cart with a TV set on it.

"Class," said Ms. Diz. "Ms. Bunelli has brought us a DVD of an amazing tap dancer. I think you're going to enjoy this!"

Ms. Bunelli pushed some buttons on the DVD player.

And suddenly, there on the TV, was a man tap-dancing!

Rat-tat-tat BOUNCE!

Rat-tat-tat BOUNCE!

"Hey, that guy is a guy!" Wyatt said.

The tapping man spun and jumped and tapped so fast it made my eyes *and* my ears dizzy.

Rat-tat-TAT!

He whirled faster and faster—and got louder and louder.

RATATATTATATATTATATAT!

I never dreamed feet could make so much noise!

"Those tap shoes are the best," I whispered to Emma. "If I had those, I would tap twenty-four hours a day!"

"You should take tap dance with me," Emma whispered back. "We'd have so much fun together!"

My very own noisy shoes?

"Emma," I said, "you are a genius."

6
The King of Tap

It took a while to convince Mom and Dad I really wanted to take tap dance lessons.

When I brought it up at dinner that night, they both made sighing noises.

"Remember when you wanted to take pottery?" Mom asked.

"Or karate?" Dad said.

"Or ice skating?" Mom added.

"I didn't know it would be so cold at the skating rink," I said.

"Roscoe," Dad said. "You promised you would stick to those things. And you quit every time."

"This time it'll be different, Dad," I said. "I promise!"

"Can I take tap dancing with Roscoe?" my little sister, Hazel, asked. "They have pretend tap shoes at Toys Or Else."

"We'll see," said my mom.

Which is Parent for "Don't Count on It."

Max, my older brother, was balancing a lima bean on his nose.

"Roscoe, are you sure about tap dance?" he asked.

"Totally sure," I said. "Why?"

"Guys might tease you about it," Max said.

"Tease him?" said Mom. "Why?"

"Because dancing is kind of a girl thing to do is all," Max said. "Gee, Mom. Do you live in a cave or what?"

"Your Uncle Joe took ballet for a year while he was in college," Dad said. "To help him with his football footwork."

Max made a *no-way* face. "Really? Like with a frilly tutu?"

"I'm fairly certain there weren't any tutus involved," Dad said.

"Boys do so tap-dance," I said. "Ms. Diz even showed us a DVD of a tap guy. There will probably be lots of boys in my class."

Max looked up at the ceiling and groaned.

Which is Brother for "You Are Such a Doofus."

"Please can I do this?" I begged my

parents. "I absolutely promise I won't quit this time."

Mom looked at Dad. Dad looked at Mom.

My parents have entire conversations without ever opening their mouths.

"I suppose you could give it a try," Mom said finally. "But I want you to stick with it, no matter what."

"I will!" I cried. "I will for sure stick!"

"Can I have Roscoe's tap shoes when he quits?" Hazel asked.

"We'll see," said Mom.

"Don't hold your breath, Hazel," I said. "Because I am going to tap dance FOR-EVER!"

That weekend, Mom found some tap shoes at a yard sale.

They weren't all shiny and new like Emma's.

But they were just as loud.

I practiced tapping on the kitchen

floor. (Great taps!)

The living room carpet. (Crummy taps.)

My bed. (No taps. But terrific bounces.)

And the bathtub.

You get LOUD taps out of a bathtub, let me tell you.

I decided it was my favorite place to tap.

My mom decided I was going to have to clean the bathtub.

But it was worth it.

I was a tapping fool. A crazy tapping machine.

I was going to love, *love*, LOVE tap dancing!

Forever.

7

Surrounded

Finally it was time for my very first tap lesson.

Emma's mom drove us there.

The tap dance place was an old brick building. It had a sign that said TRIXIE'S TIP-TOP TAP STUDIO.

We were a little late. So Emma and I ran inside as fast as we could.

24

A lady with her gray hair in a twisty circle on her head was standing near the door.

She had on a black skirt and shiny tap shoes with bright red bows.

"Emma! Slow down, dear! We are just about to start class," said the lady.

"Miss Trixie, this is Roscoe Riley," Emma said. "He's new."

"Wonderful!" said Miss Trixie. "I am ecstatic to have an enthusiastic young gentleman like yourself join our ranks!"

I looked at Emma. She likes big words more than I do.

"She's glad to have you in the class," she explained.

"Oh," I said. "I'm glad to have me in the class too."

We followed Miss Trixie into a giant room.

The shiny wooden floor looked just like the one in the school gym. One wall was made of mirrors.

I waved to myself.

Emma and I rushed to a bench by the wall and put on our tap shoes.

The air was full of *clicks* and *clacks*.

Miss Trixie clapped her hands.

"Tappers! Let the glorious fun begin!" she cried.

"That means it's time to get in line," said

Emma. "Stand next to me."

Miss Trixie went to the middle of the room.

"Ladies," she said, "I am most delighted to introduce the newest member of our tap team, Mr. Roscoe Riley! Roscoe, take a bow, won't you?" Miss Trixie asked.

My face got hot. But I bowed.

As I straightened up, I saw myself in the wall of mirrors.

I saw my tap shoes. And my ears that

stick out a little too much.

I saw my pink cheeks. And my striped shirt and my nice worn-in jeans.

I saw a long row of tappers.

I saw tall tappers and freckled tappers and tappers with missing teeth.

But there was one thing I did not see.

I did not see one single other boy.

8

The Gentleman

I was in a totally guyless room.

A boy-free zone.

A sea of pink.

"Why didn't you tell me there aren't any boys in this class?" I whispered to Emma.

Emma looked surprised. "Does it matter?"

"Yes, it matters!" I whispered back.

I wasn't even exactly sure *why* it mattered.

Except that it meant maybe Max had been right, after all.

Maybe tap dancing was For Girls Only.

That meant kids at school would tease me.

Bully-breath Wyatt already had a long list of bully nicknames for me.

I did not need to have him add another one.

"Let's start with some heel-toes," Miss Trixie said.

I raised my hand. "Miss Trixie?"

"Yes, dear?"

"I . . . uh . . ." I swallowed. "I'm going to sit on the bench for a minute. There's a stone in my shoe, I think."

"By all means!" she said.

I sat down on a bench and yanked off one of my tap shoes.

Tinkly music filled the room.

"Let's start with our dance called 'The Mice and the Elephants'!" said Miss Trixie.

The girls began to tap their toes.

"Twinkle toes! Twinkle toes!" Miss Trixie said. "Tip-tap! Tip-tap!"

While she twinkled, Emma looked over her shoulder at me.

"Are you okay?" she asked.

I nodded.

But I wasn't okay.

I was the only boy in a gigantic roomful of girls.

I pretended to look for a rock in my shoe.

"Let's heel-toe in a circle, lovely little

mice!" Miss Trixie called.

Everyone tiptoed. All those clicks made a wonderful sound.

The music changed. It got slow and loud and thumpy.

"Time for the elephants!" called Miss Trixie. "Clomp and stomp like glorious pachyderms!"

I watched Emma stamp her tap shoes. She swung her arms together like a long trunk.

If *pachyderm* meant "elephant" in normal language, then Emma was being a great one.

Slowly I put my tap shoe back on.

I tried out a few clomps while I sat on the bench.

It was hard *not* to clomp, with all that *thump, thump, thumping* elephant music.

It felt good to make so much noise and

not even get yelled at.

"Roscoe? Will you be joining us today?" Miss Trixie called.

I didn't answer right away.

But finally I said, "I guess a little clomping couldn't hurt."

I ran over and joined the circle of girls.

I tried out some mouse tiptoes.

"Excellent, Mr. Riley!" said Miss Trixie. "Now try the pachyderm part!"

I clomped and swung and tiptoed and twinkled.

"A glorious job!" said Miss Trixie. "And it was nice to have the addition of our fine new gentleman tapper!"

My face got a little hot again.

But I didn't mind so much.

We learned more steps during the rest of the class.

My favorite step was called STOMP-STOMP-CLAP.

I had such a good time making noise, I almost forgot about being the only gentleman in a roomful of girls.

When the lesson was over, Emma and I took off our tap shoes and put our regular ones back on.

"So?" Emma said. "What do you think?"

"It was awesome," I said.

"Does that mean you're going to keep coming? Even if you're the only guy?"

I thought. But only for a mini second.

"You better believe it!" I said.

"I'm glad," said Emma.

"Me too," I said.

To celebrate, we did a high five.

With our tap shoes on our hands.

9

Emma's Question

The next day at circle time, Ms. Diz made an announcement.

"Class," she said, "this morning I put a sign-up sheet on the bulletin board. The whole school is having a celebration for Mrs. Herman in a couple weeks. She's retiring at the end of the school year."

Mrs. Herman is one of the kindergarten teachers.

She is about one hundred and sixty years old.

"Do you realize that Mrs. Herman has been a teacher here for thirty-seven years?" asked Ms. Diz.

She closed her eyes for a moment. "Wow. Imagine that! Thirty. Seven. Years."

She looked a little woozy when she opened her eyes.

"Anyway," she went on, "we're going to have a talent show as part of the celebration. That's what the sign-up sheet is for."

Emma nudged me with her elbow.

"Roscoe, you know what I was thinking?" she whispered.

"Nope," I said.

Half the time I don't even know what *I'm* thinking.

"You and I could enter the talent show. We could do 'The Mice and the Elephants' dance."

I thought about being the only boy in Miss Trixie's class.

"Please?" Emma begged. "Mrs. Herman

was my kindergarten teacher and she was the best. I really want to be in her show!"

I thought about the tap-dancing guy on the DVD Ms. Diz had shown our class.

And then I thought about being the loudest elephant in the history of elephants.

"PLEASE?" Emma looked at me with a hopeful, we're-best-buddies face.

How could I say no?

"Okay," I agreed.

"Emma and Roscoe," Ms. Diz said. "Is there something you want to share with the class?"

That is Teacher for "Your mouths are open when they are supposed to be closed."

"Sorry, Ms. Diz," said Emma. "We were just deciding to enter the talent show. As tap dancers."

Wyatt made a pig-snort laugh. "*Roscoe's*

going to dance? Will he be wearing a tutu?"

"That's just for ballet dancers," I said. "And tap dancers get to make lots of noise. It's way fun."

"I think it's wonderful that you want to be in the show," said Ms. Diz. "You two will make a great addition."

I watched Emma go over to the bulletin board and sign our names.

Then I rolled my eyes at Wyatt.

Which is like sticking out your tongue with your eyeballs.

I decided that having Wyatt make fun of me wasn't so bad.

After all, I was used to it.

Besides, nobody else had laughed at the idea of me being a tap dancer.

Max was probably wrong about that

whole teasing thing.

Max is almost always wrong.

Emma came back to the circle doing a heel-toe on the carpet.

"We're all signed up," she said. "I'm so excited! This is going to be a blast!"

She looked so happy and sure that I felt happy and sure too.

Unlike Max, Emma is almost always right.

10

Dancing Girls

At our next lesson, Miss Trixie said we could borrow her "Mice and Elephants" music CD for the talent show.

We decided that Emma would dance the mouse part for the talent show. And I would be the elephant.

Because I am a talented stomper.

Every chance I got, I practiced my stomping.

I practiced stomping so much that Dad said maybe he would have to send my tap shoes on a long vacation to somewhere very far away.

I practiced so much that when the morning of the talent show came, I wasn't even hardly nervous.

On the playground that morning, Emma and I worked on our dance.

Even though our tap shoes were in our cubbies, we hummed the music while we tapped on the blacktop near the basketball court.

Gus watched us while he swung from the monkey bars.

When we were done, he yelled, "Way to go! Do it again, guys!"

We tapped again.

"Mrs. Herman is going to love this," Emma said. "I can't wait until she sees us!"

Some other kids gathered to watch.

It was kind of fun, having an audience.

We tapped and stomped and twinkled.

When one of us had a solo part, the other one stood and watched.

You could tell whose turn it was from the sound of the music.

My elephant part was loud and stompy.

Emma's mouse part was quiet and twinkly.

"Look at the two little dancing girls!" someone yelled.

Two older boys were staring at us.

And laughing.

In that special mean way only big boys know how to do.

"No, wait! One of the girls is a guy!" said the biggest big boy.

"Twinkle-toes over there? No way! That is a girl for sure!" said the other one.

Gus jumped off the monkey bars.

"Of course he's a guy!" he yelled back. "He has short hair and his name is Roscoe. DUH."

The boys just laughed and walked off.

It was nice to have Gus defend me.

But suddenly I felt exactly like I had those first few minutes at Miss Trixie's.

When I'd realized I was a guy surrounded by a gigantic roomful of tapping people who were definitely *not* guys.

Ms. Diz walked over. "Roscoe," she said, "I hope you'll ignore those comments. You understand that tap dance is for girls *and* boys, right?"

"I guess," I said quietly.

Emma was watching me with her worried face.

"I'm kind of pooped out from practicing," I said. "I think I'll go swing for a while, Emma."

I headed for the swings.

It was one thing to get teased by Wyatt.

He makes fun of everybody.

But those big guys would be in the audience that afternoon.

Along with lots of other big guys.

Maybe even bigger guys.

I started swinging.

And thought.

I swung higher and higher.

I liked being an elephant.

But I didn't like getting teased.

It was okay for Emma. Nobody was

going to make fun of her.

The bell rang.

I watched the classes start forming their lines.

I could see the big boys getting ready to go into their classroom. They were laughing their mean laughs again.

I had to get out of dancing. Somehow.

I made a decision.

My conscience was going to give me trouble on this one.

That's the naggy little person who lives in your brain and makes you feel guilty about stuff.

Man, I hate that guy sometimes.

I jumped off the swing.

I landed on the soft stuff they put on the ground around the swings and monkey bars.

But instead of walking away, I rolled

onto the ground.

"OW!" I cried. "OW OW OW!"

"Roscoe, what's wrong?" Ms. Diz asked.

She ran over and knelt down beside me.

"I fell off the swing and I think I broke something!" I said.

"Where does it hurt?" Ms. Diz asked.

"Everywhere," I said.

I looked at Emma.

Especially my conscience, I thought.

11

Nurse Oshkosh

Ms. Diz helped me limp to the nurse's office.

When I sat down in a green plastic chair, I remembered to groan a little.

"I'll go find the nurse," said Ms. Diz. "Roscoe, you stay put."

While she was gone, I thought about what injuries I needed.

They would have to be bad enough to get me out of the talent show.

Not *ambulance* bad.

But bad enough to get me a nice pair of crutches.

It wouldn't be easy.

I knew Ms. Vasquez, the nurse.

She'd been a nurse a long time. She could spot a faker a mile away.

The door opened.

I closed my eyes. I groaned and grabbed my busted leg.

I groaned so well that even *I* believed me.

"Here's the patient," said Ms. Diz. "Roscoe, I'll check on you in a while, sweetie."

I opened my eyes.

Where was Ms. Vasquez?

A *man* was standing there!

He was tall and skinny, with one of the heart-hearing death-o-scopes around his neck.

A doctor? This was bad news.

Doctors had X-ray machines.

They could look inside and tell when you were faking.

Kind of like moms.

"You're not Ms. Vasquez," I said.

"She's got a cold," the man said.

"I don't need a whole doctor. A nurse will be plenty, I think."

The man smiled.

"I *am* a nurse, Roscoe. My name's John Oshkosh."

I accidentally laughed.

"Which part are you laughing at?" he asked. "My name or my job?"

"Both," I admitted.

"No problem," he said. "I get that a lot."

"But you're a *guy*."

"Lots of guys are named John," he said.

"No. I meant . . . you know. The nurse part," I said.

"Lots of guys are nurses."

"But it's kind of a girl job, isn't it?" I asked.

Mr. Oshkosh looked surprised. "I've always just thought it was a great job."

I felt kind of bad, pointing out that he was in the wrong line of work.

But I figured someone should have let him in on that information by now.

"Let's take a look," said Mr. Oshkosh. "Where does it hurt?"

"Everywhere," I said.

I remembered to groan again.

"My left leg is broken, I think," I added. "And my right elbow and my left appendix."

I did not know what an appendix was exactly.

But I figured a broken one might need some crutches.

"Hmm." Mr. Oshkosh looked at me. "You're going to be a complicated case."

"Are you *sure* you're a nurse?" I asked.

He sat down next to me on a rolling stool.

"Yep. Went to nurse school and everything."

He gently moved my leg up and down.

"OWWW," I cried.

"You said it was your left leg," said Mr. Oshkosh. "That's your right."

"Actually, I think I may have busted my whole body," I said.

He thought for a minute. "A busted body, eh? We may have to send you to the hospital for X-rays."

"NO!" I cried. "I can tell it's not an X-ray kind of busted. Probably I'll be better in one day. Or even in a couple hours."

Mr. Oshkosh looked at me carefully. "Ms. Diz tells me you were supposed to be in the talent show this afternoon."

I hung my head to show how sad I was. "I really wanted to tap-dance."

He nodded. "It would be hard to dance with crutches. I guess your dance partner will have to go on alone. You think she'll be okay?"

"Well, there are two different dancing parts," I said. "But I think so."

I hope so, I thought.

"You think some crutches will take care of your busted body?" Mr. Oshkosh asked.

"Oh, yeah. Although some gigantic white bandages would be nice too."

"Bandages," he repeated.

I tilted my head at him. "Are you POSITIVE you're a nurse? Because you don't sound real sure about what's wrong with me."

Mr. Oshkosh patted my shoulder. "I know exactly what's wrong," he said. "I've been there, kid."

Mr. Oshkosh didn't give me any bandages.

But he did give me a nice pair of crutches.

Those are way fun. Once you get the hang of them.

"You're a great nurse," I told Mr. Oshkosh.

"Thanks," he said. "You're a great patient. I'll walk you back to Ms. Diz's class."

When we reached my classroom, Mr. Oshkosh said, "Roscoe, if you need anything, let me know. And tell your friend I'm sorry she lost her dance partner."

"Yeah," I said quietly. "I will."

"You can head into class. But before you go, there's one thing I want you to remember."

"Yes?" I asked.

He pointed to my right leg. I was holding it off the ground so it would look smushed.

"It's your LEFT leg, buddy. Not your right."

12
Crutching

I crutched into class.

Everybody stared at me as I made my way to my desk.

I showed all the kids how to use my crutches.

I told them about my busted body. And how I'd have to miss the talent show.

I didn't look at Emma when I said that part.

While I let some of the other kids try my crutches, Emma came over.

"I'm really sorry about your accident," she said. "Does it hurt a lot?"

"Not so much," I said. "I'm sad about the show, though."

"I really wanted to dance for Mrs. Herman," Emma said.

"Wait a minute, Emma," I said. "Just because I can't dance doesn't mean that you shouldn't."

Emma sighed. "How can I be a dancing elephant *and* a dancing mouse? It will look silly."

"No it won't!" I said.

I felt pretty bad. I never thought that my crutches would keep Emma from dancing. And I knew how much she liked Mrs. Herman.

"Come on, Emma," I said. "You can do it!"

"I guess I could just dance the mouse part," Emma said.

"That's great!" I said. "I mean—you'll be great!"

Emma looked at me a long time.

She has black, smart eyes.

They're the kind of eyes that can see inside you.

Just like a doctor with an X-ray machine.

. . .

By afternoon time, I was kind of tired of those crutches.

After a while with those pokey sticks, your armpits get awfully sore.

It took me a long time to crutch to the talent show in the auditorium.

Right in front of the stage there was a big table with flowers and cookies on it. Mrs. Herman was sitting there.

"My goodness, Roscoe," she said as I crutched past. "What on earth happened to you?"

"I busted my body," I said.

Mrs. Herman gave me a gentle hug. "You watch yourself, you old rascal."

I nodded. I didn't know what to say.

It felt like a cheating hug I didn't really deserve.

"You watch your old rascal self too," I said at last.

Ms. Diz showed us the row of chairs where our class was going to sit.

"Those of you who are going to be in the talent show, follow me backstage," she said.

Thomas and Coco and Emma started to go.

Thomas was going to whistle "Skip to My Lou" on his skateboard.

And Coco was going to sing a Raffi song.

Coco does not sing very in tune.

But she makes up for it with loudness.

I started to follow Emma backstage.

"Roscoe," said Ms. Diz. "You can stay here, since you're not going to be dancing."

"But what if Emma gets nervous or something?" I asked.

"All right, then." Ms. Diz waved for me to come along.

Slowly I crutched my way up to the stage.

Behind the giant red curtain, lots of kids were warming up for their acts.

Emma tied on her tap shoes. She'd

brought mine along too.

"They were in your cubby," she said. "I don't know why I brought them. Guess I was hoping for a miracle cure."

She poked her head out from behind the curtain.

When she pulled back, her eyes were scared.

"There's too many people!" she whispered.

I peeked out too.

I saw Mrs. Herman and Ms. Diz and my class and Max's class and the principal and Mr. Oshkosh.

Mr. Oshkosh gave me a wave.

Then he pointed to his leg.

His LEFT leg.

I yanked my head back in.

"It's not so many people, really," I said.

"Just the whole school."

Sometimes I do not exactly have a way with words.

The crowd got very quiet.

I peeked out again.

Mr. Goosegarden, the principal, was standing near the edge of the stage.

"We are here today," he said, "to honor the career of our wonderful teacher, Mrs. Herman."

His voice got a little lower. "Let me remind you that it takes a lot of courage to step onstage in front of an audience. I want you to give these talented students the respect they deserve."

He went on for a while longer.

Speeching is probably the main job of principals.

At last the show got started.

Emma and I watched from the side of the stage.

We laughed when some kids in the pre-K class jumped on bubbles while music played.

It was an unusual talent, for sure.

But mostly we just watched without talking.

We watched the baton twirler.

And the girl who could stand on her head for two minutes.

And the boy who said "Pick a card, any card" to Mrs. Herman, but then he couldn't guess which one she'd picked until he got halfway through the deck.

We watched. And we clapped.

And we waited for it to be Emma's turn.

It was a long, quiet, guilty wait.

13
Twinkles and Clomps

Finally it was time.

The CD player came on with our "Mice and Elephants" music.

The curtain opened.

Emma swallowed. Then she tapped across the stage.

I leaned on my crutches and crossed my fingers.

The music was loud and echoey.

Boy, that was a giant audience.

From the stage, it looked like a monster with too many heads.

When the tinkly mouse part of the music played, Emma made teensy tapping steps.

She even smiled a little.

When the elephant part of the music played, Emma just stood there. Waiting.

Since I wasn't there to stomp.

To tell you the truth, it did look just a little bit silly.

You could tell an elephant was supposed to be on the stage too.

The elephant stomping part stopped. The tinkly music came back.

And Emma started dancing her mouse part again.

She was tapping her heart out.

Being the very best mouse she could be.

And I was hiding behind a curtain.

Being a chicken.

The elephant music came back.

Emma stopped tapping.

She wasn't smiling anymore. In fact, she

looked a little sad.

I could hear kids whispering, and I thought about the big boys watching Emma dance all alone.

Without an elephant in sight.

I dropped my crutches.

I kicked off my sneakers.

I shoved on my tap shoes.

And I tapped right onto that stage.

Emma stared at me. Her mouth made an O shape.

I think maybe she was in chalk.

That's when you can't believe what your eyes are saying.

"I'm cured!" I whispered. "It's a miracle!"

The elephant music played on.

I clomped like a pro.

The mouse music played.

Emma twinkle-tapped like she'd been dancing forever.

We tapped and clapped and twirled.

I was so busy making noise with my feet, I forgot all about the big boys.

I forgot all about my busted body and my broken left appendix.

I forgot all about whether tap dancing was just for girls or just for boys or maybe just for everybody.

I also forgot all about the edge of the stage.

I twinkle-tapped right off that stage like a giant flying mouse-elephant-boy.

I probably would have busted my whole body for real.

If I'd landed on the floor.

But lucky for me, old Mrs. Herman saved the day!

Her guest-of-honor table was right next to the stage.

So instead of the floor, I landed on her table.

And her. A little bit.

I knocked over her coffee cup and crumbled her cookies.

But I just kept on tapping away.

Because the show must go on.

Mrs. Herman kept saying, "Oh, my! Oh, my!"

Maybe she was just amazed at my fancy footwork.

Or maybe it was because I sort of tapped on her sweater sleeve a couple times.

Finally the music ended and it was time for our bows.

I did a great one. Except I sort of got tangled in my tap-shoe ties.

And plopped right into Mrs. Herman's lap.

Everybody clapped like crazy.

I looked up at Emma on the stage.

She waved at me and smiled.

Then she did an elephant clomp, just for fun.

She made a glorious pachyderm.

14

Good-Bye from Time-Out

That evening, Mrs. Herman called my house.

She asked my mom how my busted body was.

After that, I had a little bit of explaining to do.

Mom called Mr. Oshkosh after I told her the whole story.

I told him I was sorry for faking a smushed body.

He said he'd had a feeling I would make a full recovery.

Dad and Mom talked to me for a long time.

About how I should do what makes me happy.

Not what other people think is right for me.

And they explained how there's no such thing as boy stuff or girl stuff.

Then I explained that sometimes they make me more confused when they are trying to un-confuse me.

Especially when it's complicated things like boys and girls.

Dad said not to worry. Because he's still trying to figure that stuff out.

Mom laughed. Then she threw a pillow at him.

Sitting here in time-out, I have figured out one thing, at least.

I'm going to take lots more tap classes.

And guess what?

After the show, Dewan and Gus both asked me how they could sign up for tap lessons.

And Wyatt actually asked if he could try my tap shoes on.

So I let him.

He said he wanted to see if the tappers would be good for smushing ants.

But I could tell he liked that *clickety-clack* noise as much as I do.

Well, *almost* as much.

I like it so much I am going to keep taking dance lessons forever and ever, I think.

Emma says she will too.

She was right about how much fun we'd have.

Emma is almost always right.

10 NOISES I REALLY LOVE

by Me, Roscoe Riley

1. New sneakers squeaking
   on the gym floor

2. Skateboards racing
   down the sidewalk

3. Frog croaks

4. Lion roars

5. Cat purrs

6. Drums in a marching band

7. Thunder
   (when your mom and dad are with you)

8. Fireworks
   (when your mom and dad are with you)

9. Tap dancing in a mud puddle

10. Tap dancing anywhere!

Turn the page for a
super-special sneak peek
at MY next adventure!

ROSCOE RILEY

RULES #6

Never Walk in Shoes that Talk

Everything started one morning, when I was putting my backpack in my cubby at school.

I heard Gus shout my name.

"Roscoe! You gotta see this! Hassan and Coco have talking shoes!"

Gus grabbed my arm and pulled. "Come on! This is major!"

Gus says lots of crazy things.

Once he told me he was pretty sure his guinea pig could count to ten in Spanish.

So when he told me two kids in our class had talking shoes, I wasn't all that surprised.

"They're called Walkie-Talkies," Gus said. "I saw them on TV. You will not believe the amazingness of these shoes!"

We ran into class.

And there before me was a whole new world of shoe possibilities.

Kids surrounded Hassan and Coco, who were each wearing a kind of sneaker I'd never seen before.

The shoes were made of shiny plastic. Like the boots my sister wears when it rains.

On one shoe was a big *W*.

On the other shoe was a big *T*.

There was a black push button near the toe of each shoe.

Coco's sneakers were pink. With glitter shoelaces.

Hassan's sneakers were blue with lightning stripes.

Coco and Hassan were sitting in chairs on opposite sides of the room.

Coco had her left leg crossed over her knee.

She was whispering something into her shoe.

Which I have to admit looked pretty weird.

Hassan had his right leg crossed over his knee.

And here's the can-you-believe-it thing— Coco's voice was coming out of Hassan's shoe!

"See?" Gus whispered. "Walkie-Talkies! You talk into that little circle on the left shoe. It's sort of like talking into a cell phone. And if you have a friend with a pair of Walkie-Talkies on, they can hear you out of a little bitty speaker in their right toe!"

I did not even know what to say.

It was a science miracle.

Better even than Silly Putty.

Coco whispered something to her foot.

Hassan's shoe said, "I just LOVE my Walkie-Talkies!"

Hassan's shoe.

Coco's voice.

Hassan grinned. "My dad got mine in Los Angeles on a business trip. Last time he just brought me a pack of peanuts and a cocktail napkin."

"Wow," I said.

"Yeah," Hassan agreed. "The only bad

thing is that they are kind of uncomfort-able. I have three blisters already."

"I have four," Coco said.

We sat there, ooh-ing and ahh-ing.

I knew what we were all thinking.

We were wondering what we could say to our parents that might make *them* say, "Hmm, this kid is so sweet I think I will run to the nearest store and buy him some Walkie-Talkies before they are all sold out."

I tried hard to think of something sweet to tell my dad.

He is getting balder every day.

Maybe I could tell him I'd noticed some fresh hair sprouts.

Katherine Applegate has never owned tap shoes, but she likes the clickety sound they make. She can do an excellent bubble-gum pop, and recently learned how to make armpit farts using a straw.* Katherine lives in a very noisy household in California, with her husband, two kids, and assorted pets.

* Place bendy straw in armpit. Blow. Enjoy.

Welcome to Roscoe Riley's world

of mishaps, mistakes, and way cool misadventures!

From bestselling author Katherine Applegate

ROSCOE RILEY Rules #1
Never Glue Your Friends to Chairs
Katherine Applegate
illustrated by Brian Biggs

ROSCOE RILEY Rules 2
Never Swipe a Bully's Bear
Katherine Applegate
illustrated by Brian Biggs

ROSCOE RILEY Rules 3
Don't Swap Your Sweater for a Dog
Katherine Applegate
illustrated by Brian Biggs

ROSCOE RILEY Rules 4
Never Swim in Applesauce
Katherine Applegate
illustrated by Brian Biggs

ROSCOE RILEY Rules #
Don't Tap-Dance on Your Teacher
Katherine Applegate
illustrated by Brian Biggs

HarperCollins*Children's Books*
www.harpercollinschildrens.com